The Hired Gun

The Hired Gun

a novella by
Bob MacKenzie

Dark Matter Press
Kingston, Canada

Library and Archives Canada Cataloguing in Publication

MacKenzie, Bob, 1947-
The hired gun : a novella / by Bob MacKenzie.

ISBN 978-0-9916858-7-5 (paperback)

I. Title.

PS8575.K424H57 2016   jC813'.6   C2016-900280-2

The Hired Gun
cover & interior
illustrations by
Mike St. Pierre

In 1959, western Canada was only half a century removed from the old west that was already being commemorated in books and in movies and television series. Cowboys and oilmen dominated the popular imagination in this rural economy of prairie towns surrounded by small family farms. The culture was in gradual transition, with an eye to the future but with one foot planted firmly in the previous century. The new mythology of the old west fueled the imagination of every child bored by an uneventful hot and dry Alberta summer.

Chapter 1

June is a slow month in Elizabeth, even now. With most crops in and harvest some time off, commerce slows to a standstill. When I was twelve, it seemed even slower. In the summer of 1959 the signs on the outskirts of town read "Elizabeth, Alberta, Pop. 993." In a town of a thousand people, even a twelve year old knows just about everyone, and the arrival of a stranger can become an event. We were ready, that summer, for something to happen.

Unlike the farm kids, we rarely had even chores to fill our time. Sometimes we would walk or ride our bikes to the reservoir, about a mile and a half outside town, where we would strip to our underwear and swim in the sunwarmed water. Sometimes we would ride the mile out to the Highway Service Station on Highway 3, to play the jukebox and sip Coke alongside the farmers and truckdrivers who would stop in for a break. Other times we would ride around the country roads, looking for pop or beer bottles to sell, stopping once in a while to cool off in the water of a farmer's dugout, our toes sinking in the soft clay and dung deposited by the cattle we shared the water with. Often we would visit the dump outside town, looking for what we called "good stuff," items we could use, or old batteries and copper wire we could sell to old Sweeney, the junk man. Mostly though, we just hung around the Chinaman's or the Crown Hotel, drinking Coke, eating chips, and listening to the juke box.

We were hanging around the Crown the day the stranger came to town, me and Alex, Dickie and Linda and Sam. Sam was a girl, but someone slapped that name on her and it stuck. So there we were, sitting around the box, when that big black car pulled up outside. Through the windows of the café, we could see the driver get out.

He had a city look about him, a man perhaps around my father's age then, about thirty or thirty five, in a charcoal suit with a tie of the richest maroon. He looked nowhere in particular as he stepped out of the car, yet I felt he had seen all that was around him.

"Looks like a funeral director," Sam giggled. We all laughed. Standing there in that dark suit beside that big Lincoln in the hot sun, he did look a lot like Mr. Harley, who owned the funeral parlour over in Mountbatten.

He looked like a movie star too, his hair all teased back and feathered, but not long like the ducktails the Callahan boys wore, and his mustache neatly trimmed. Dapper, my mother would have called him. A movie star, I thought, not a funeral director. But I didn't say it.

He walked past the window toward the hotel entrance, and our interest shifted elsewhere.

It was later the talk started, about who he might be and what he was doing in Elizabeth. I suppose because we had nothing much else to do, and because watching a stranger in town seemed somehow mysterious and exciting, we kids seemed to know his every move. Yet how much could we really have known that long ago day, of what was to come?

That evening after supper we rode our bikes out to the reservoir. Besides me and Alex there Linda and Sam came along too. At twelve, we were just beginning to discover the opposite sex. We would go somewhere quiet, like the poplar grove by the reservoir, and we would experiment with necking. We would pair off at random and try the fleeting kiss, the hesitant touch of hands. Anything more serious would have terrified us worse than if we had found a dead body.

We had just settled into a leafy patch of ground in the poplar grove when we heard two men arguing. We crept to the edge of the grove and peered out across the reservoir. Mr. Paulins was facing almost directly at us. The other man had his back to us, but by his gruff voice and the large mustache on his silhouette, we figured him to be Mr. Dutka, the manager of the Co-op Store. Although it was loud, most of what they said was lost on the prairie wind, mixed with the song of frogs and crickets around the water.

He had a city look about him, a man perhaps around my father's age then, about thirty or thirty five, in a charcoal suit with a tie of the richest maroon. He looked nowhere in particular as he stepped out of the car, yet I felt he had seen all that was around him.

All we could tell was they were angry. Both of them.
Then Mr. Dutka grabbed Mr. Paulins by the collar and
leaned in close. He said something real quiet. Mr.
Paulins pulled loose and walked away. He yelled back
over his shoulder, but we only heard part of it clearly.

"...tell him everything! You'll see!"

After that, both men got in their cars, which were
parked over the other side of the reservoir, and drove
back toward town. Then it was quiet again.

"Gosh," was all Alex said, but I could tell he was
thinking again, making things bigger than they
probably really were, as he tended to do. The rest of us
were quiet.

Sam placed her hand softly on mine, but necking
was hard work and the argument had somehow broken
the mood. I got up and led her back to our bikes. Alex
and Linda followed us. Just before we got on our bikes,
and without us even planning it, Sam kissed me right
on the lips. Then she was on her bike and gone down
the road.

The next morning, Sam and I went out riding
together. Alex was helping his dad out with something
at the garage, so I had nothing better to do.

At least, that is what I told myself. In fact, even at
just twelve, I rather enjoyed the company of a young
lady. And Sam was a pretty young girl, a young woman
really, sensual in her bluejeans and pink blouse with
the breeze just slightly blowing her shoulder length
hair.

We had been out about an hour when we decided to take a run down the dump road. We were way out near the last bend when Sam cried out.

"Bobby, look!"

He stood there in the middle of the gravel road, staring us down defiantly–a young hawk.

"Stop, Sam."

We had both already applied the brakes, and we stopped very near the hawk, who was now hopping away from us. One wing flapped; the other hung limply, only occasionally attempting to move.

"He's hurt."

"Let's get him, Sam. We'll take him to Doc Stevens."

The road turned into a whirlwind of dust as we both scurried after the bird and it scuttled and flopped and flapped to escape us. The needle sharp claws grabbed at us and the razor sharp bill bit at us each time we grabbed him, forcing us to let go or bleed. Finally, I got behind him and held his wings to his side with one hand while keeping his head straight with the other.

"The bag! Get the bag."

I always had a paper bag in the basket of my bike, for bottles and such. Now, we placed the bird as gently as was safe into that bag. Then we rode our bikes back to town, to the veterinarian's office.

It was Doc Stevens told us it looked like the bird had been shot. Most likely a kid with a twenty two, he said, although the hole was big for a twenty two. He said the bird was lucky we found it. He also said it was lucky to survive a ride back in a paper bag. We had saved a life together and I always felt closer to Sam after that. She

I got up and led her back to our bikes. Alex and Linda followed us. Just before we got on our bikes, and without us even planning it, Sam kissed me right on the lips. Then she was on her bike and gone down the road.

had been almost as brave as a boy in capturing that bird.

When we went by the garage to tell him, Alex figured he could have done as well. He also had his own theory about how the bird got shot.

"It was him did it."

"Who, Alex?"

"Him. Mr. Black Lincoln. For practice."

Sam and I laughed. Alex was always getting these ideas about people. He was mostly wrong.

Chapter 2

It was Alex and I saw him walk into the Treasury Branch office and make a deposit. We stood at the windows, peering in at this dark stranger as he did his business inside.

"Wow, will ya look at that, Bobby! Must be about a million dollars!"

Alex always did tend to exaggerate a bit.

"Not quite," I replied, "but it sure is a whole lot of money."

In the wicket between the stranger and the teller was a pile of bundled twenty dollar bills, way more than either of us had ever seen at one time before. He had taken them from his briefcase to make his deposit. I was curious, to say the least.

"Let's see where he goes," I said.

"Sure," said Alex, but he sounded unsure of himself.

"What's the matter? You chicken?"

"Nah, it's not that. It's just...."

"Come on. He won't hurt you. Let's see what he's up to."

And just at that point, the man came out the door and began walking up First Avenue toward Main Street a half block away. Alex just swallowed quickly and we both followed behind. Our quarry turned on Main Street and walked to Paulins' store, which he entered.

When we looked in the big front windows, the man was already at the cash register talking to Mr. Paulins. Well, it looked to us like maybe they were arguing some, because the man banged his fist hard on the counter and Mr. Paulins was waving his arms around the way he did when he got angry with one of the kids. And we could hear a mumble of their voices through the glass.

I walked in. I was pretty sure Alex was somewhere behind me.

"...hold out on me, Paulin. Or you'll regret it!"

The bell above the door announced Alex and me. Both men went quiet and turned to look at us.

"I'll talk to you later, Mr. Paulins," was all the man said, and he walked out. Alex and I bought some candy. Mr. Paulins looked tired I thought.

Alex was very quiet until we left the store.

"You see that? You see, Bobby?"

"See what?"

"When he turned to leave. Under his coat."

"No. What are you talking about?"

"A gun, Bobby. The guy has a gun."

"Are you crazy, Alex?"

"No. Really, he has a shoulder holster. Just like The Untouchables!"

"You saw that?"

"Yeah. A gun."

Like a lot of towns in Alberta, Elizabeth was too small to afford a full time policeman, so we had a Mountie instead. Town council had a contract with the RCMP detachment in Mountbatten to have a constable live in Elizabeth. Tom Porter was young and tall and blond, the idol of every girl in town, the hero of every young boy. He was everything we knew a Mountie must be.

The next day, when Alex and I saw Constable Porter standing at the corner of First and Main, apparently watching the stranger walking into the Rexall Drugstore down on Main, we stopped to talk.

"Hi, Tom," I said. It made us feel important, the way he allowed us to use his first name like that.

"Hi, boys. What's new." His attention was only half on us, the other half still somewhere down the street. Alex sort of stood there and shuffled his feet on the wood sidewalk.

"Not much," I said.

"Stranger in town," mumbled Alex.

"Happens sometimes," said Tom.

"You keeping an eye on him?"

"Why would I do that, Alex?"

"In case."

"Come on, Alex," I said, "in case of what?"

"You know. You know, Bobby. What I saw."

"Thought you saw."

"Saw. He's got a gun, Tom. In a shoulder holster. Just like a bank robber. Or a killer."

"Now, boys, I don't want you going and starting a lot of crazy rumours. Leave police business to me, okay?"

Well, Alex was not too pleased about that, being nicely told to butt out and all, but he accepted it.

At least, I thought he had accepted it until a couple of days later when we were sitting at the Chinaman's having some chips.

"He's a killer," Alex said. Right out of the blue, he said it, and caught me totally by surprise.

"Who? Who's a killer?"

"Him. Mr. Black Lincoln. He's a killer, Bobby. A hired gun."

"Alex! You get crazier and crazier. Where do you get these ideas?"

"I've been following him. At night."

"What?"

"Come with me tonight. I'll show you. He's a killer."

Well, I knew Alex. The only way to stop him spreading rumours like that around town was to humour him. I agreed to go with him.

That night I met him at seven across the street from the Crown Hotel.

"There he is. Let's go."

The man, dressed in a black shirt, western hat, bluejeans, and cowboy boots, had walked out of the hotel and was getting in his car.

"We'll lose him."

"I know where he's going. Just get on your bike."

I did, and we followed the black Lincoln west out of town. He turned down the road to the dump. We followed, getting farther and farther behind.

By the time we wheeled quietly to a stop near the black car, the stranger was some distance away. He was picking up empty bottles and cans and setting them in a row, spaced about two feet apart along the rail fence next to the caretaker's shack.

"See. Watch him."

I was silent. The man walked away from his display of bottles, back to the car, and reached in the passenger side window. He turned, a pistol now in his hand, and fired eight rapid shots. Five bottles shattered. Three cans flew into the air.

"See, a killer," said Alex, "a hired gun."

A hired gun, Alex had called the stranger. And now we were crouched not ten feet from his big black Lincoln watching him shoot bottles and cans off the top of a fence. In the prairie dusk, in his dark clothes and with his gun blazing away without a miss, that is exactly what he looked like, a hired gun. The town dump seemed very lonely then, with just this stranger, and Alex and I seeing something we should not.

"Let's get out of here," I said.

Alex was already sliding down the hummock on which we had been resting. I followed as quickly but as quietly as I could. Just as we were picking up our bicycles, Alex kicked a bottle, which rattled its way across the rubble. I suppose the noise was little, but to me it might as well have been an atomic bomb. Alex and I froze.

In the prairie dusk, in his dark clothes and with his gun blazing away without a miss, that is exactly what he looked like, a hired gun. The town dump seemed very lonely then, with just this stranger, and Alex and I seeing something we should not.

"Hello. Is somebody there?"

We stood in near perfect silence, holding our breath, waiting.

"Who's there?"

The crunch of garbage told us he was coming our way. All I could see was that gun, blazing away without a miss.

I do not remember getting on that bike or riding away, although it must have happened that way. I was riding full speed down the gravel road beside Alex when I looked back over my shoulder at the dump. There on one of the hills in the haze of dusk was the black silhouette of a man in a cowboy hat, and in one hand a gun.

Chapter 3

Back in town, we went to the Crown for a Coke. Linda and Sam and Dickie were there already, having some chips and listening to the jukebox.

They had on "Let's Think About Living", a song about all the cowboys who die in other songs. Perhaps it was from seeing too many movies, but songs seemed to me always to be more than just background, to in fact define the current situation. I was not in the mood to hear songs about cowboys shooting people. There was a spot on the side of the box we all knew about. I walked over and banged it with my fist. The needle screeched to the end of the song and the machine reselected some rock and roll. I forget which song.

I joined Alex and the others at the table.

"What's your problem?" Dickie asked.

I looked at Alex. We were agreed. Neither of us would say anything about what we had seen.

"Nothing," Alex answered.

"Not you. Bluto here."

"What do you mean, Bluto?" I asked.

"Well, you walk in here in a huff, smashing the box, you and him both white as a sheet. What's up?"

"Nothing," I answered.

I felt uncomfortable. Looking at Alex, I could see him shift in his chair and look down at the table. We were used to sharing with our friends, not keeping things from them. Still, we both kept silent.

"Okay, have it your way. Have a chip." And he shoved the plate of chips and gravy toward me. Dickie was always easy that way. He never really pushed anything too hard.

"Thanks," I said, more for the reprieve than for the chips.

I felt a hand brush lightly against mine then pull quickly away. I glanced at Sam and she smiled. Then it was over. Somehow she had made everything all right.

Chapter 4

That was the week of the big scandal. We heard it mostly over the supper table. For our parents, it was the biggest if not best news of the summer. Someone had been stealing from the Co-op Store in Elizabeth. There were thousands of dollars worth of goods ordered but not in stock, and there was cash money missing too. Lots of it. That was the rumour anyway.

James Wyatt, Elizabeth's sheriff, had been sent an anonymous letter claiming massive thefts from the Co-op, and even insinuating that it might be an inside job.

In a town like Elizabeth, sheriff is a limited office, mostly for serving writs and so on. Older men like James Wyatt are given the job almost as an honourary position. The real police work is done by the Mounties. Wyatt passed the letter on to Tom Porter, who then forwarded it to his detachment in Mountbatten.

Besides James Wyatt and Tom Porter, and of course the writer, no one in Elizabeth knew for sure what was actually in the letter. Still, as would happen in any small prairie town in the doldrums of summer, there was a lot of guessing and a lot of talk. Soon, it seemed millions of dollars had been embezzled from the Co-op. Townspeople carefully watched everyone who worked in the store, from the lowest stock boy right up to Mr. Dutka himself. No one was above suspicion.

While the adults in town were speculating on who the thief was, and who had written that damning letter, we had other concerns, Alex and I. Who was this stranger, this city man who wore cowboy garb and practiced shooting in the town dump at dusk every night?

We had thought Tom Porter was investigating the man, but now he had this problem at the Co-op to deal with. Tom had not seemed to believe us when we told him about the gun. Why would he believe the rest of it? So Alex and I knew something we could not tell anyone, not even our best friends or the town Mountie.

I only hoped the stranger had not recognized us that night at the dump.

Chapter 5

I was reading the comics at the Recall Drug Store a couple of days later when Mr. Larsen, the pharmacist, came up behind me.

"You reading or buying, son?"

I looked up at him from my crouched position, the newest "Blackhawks" still open on my knee. From that position he was imposing with his white suit and heavy blond mustache, like Doc Holliday glowering down at me. But the smile was friendly.

"I'm, ah, just looking. Sort of."

"No looking unless you're buying. That's the rule."

"Boy's got a right to know what he's buying. Like test driving a car, right?"

Mr. Larsen laughed. The voice had come from behind him. It sounded familiar, but I was unable to place it, so I stood to see better. I found myself looking straight into the eyes of the hired gun. I froze.

"Right," I mumbled. I wanted to look away, down, anywhere, but my eyes were locked on his. They were

I looked up at him from my crouched position, the newest "Blackhawks" still open on my knee. From that position he was imposing with his white suit and heavy blond mustache, like Doc Holliday glowering down at me. But the smile was friendly.

the brightest blue I had ever seen, and they were looking right into me. I felt he could read my every thought.

The look on my face must have been quite something, because both men laughed. That broke the spell. I put "Blackhawks" back on the shelf then turned and ran out of the store. Behind me I could hear them still laughing. He had looked at me like he knew. I was not laughing.

That evening, Alex and I were crawling around the combines at Halpern's, the John Deere dealership. We often used the tractors and combines as make believe war machines, castles, and space craft. The combines were especially fun because of their elevated driver's seat, the broad, spiked intake on front and propeller-like deflector at the rear, and the large grain hopper we could climb down inside. We were huddled inside the hopper of one of these great green machines when I told Alex what had happened at the drug store.

"Wow! You think he really recognized you? You think he knows?"

"I don't know, Alex. I just don't want those eyes looking at me that way again."

"What if he does know?"

"What?"

"What if he does know?"

"I heard you. What do you mean?"

"You saw him. He's a killer. What if he decides to shut us up?"

"Kill us?"

"Uh huh."

"Wouldn't he have done it already? If he was going to, that is."

"Maybe he wasn't sure. He couldn't kill every kid in town, could he?"

"And now."

"Now he's seen you. Up close."

"You think he's sure now."

"Could be. Way you said he looked at you."

Even though we were down out of the wind, the evening chill was beginning to penetrate. Inside that grain hopper I felt deathly cold.

"What do we do now?"

"Tell Tom."

"Didn't believe us before. What makes you think he will now?"

"What else?"

"Follow him. Get proof."

"Are you crazy!"

"It's the only way. Without proof, nobody will ever believe us."

"Proof of what?"

"Whatever he's up to."

"Whatever. He's going to kill someone, that's whatever! Us. He's going to kill us when he finds out we're following him."

"Then we'll have to be real careful. What other choice do we have?"

Alex just kept quiet after that.

Chapter 6

If we were to follow the stranger day and night, the other kids would wonder what was going on. Besides, we both agreed we would need help, so that very evening at the Crown we recruited Dickie and Linda and Sam. They would help us keep track of the stranger's movements around town.

For the next several days we watched without much happening. When the man left his hotel room it was to go to the Elizabeth Café or the Chinaman's or the Crown for a meal, or down to the Rexall Drugstore to pick up a magazine, or to the Treasury Branch to take out some of the large amount of money Alex and I had seen him put in. One thing we noticed was, unlike most men over twenty one in Elizabeth, he never went to the liquor store or the bars.

Alex, as usual, was the one to explain the stranger's teetotaller habits.

"Aim," he said, "a killer has to have a steady eye and steady hands. If he misses, he may never get a second chance. The man is saving his aim. No good hired gun touches that hard liquor. At least, not when he's on the job."

There was an edge to our laughter at his flat statement. We were not all that sure he was not correct. After all, while the stranger's days were very ordinary and proper, he still went each evening to the town dump. He still practiced shooting for at least an hour daily. His aim was perfect.

Then, on Wednesday, he did not go to the dump. Earlier that day he had made a withdrawal from his Treasury Branch account, several bundles of twenties. He had placed them in his briefcase, the same one he carried when he left the hotel around eight that evening.

We had not spread out as we did during the daytime, to watch each possible direction he might travel. After all, he
would be going to the dump. We stood, the five of us with our bikes, in the space between old man Havelock's hardware store and Paulins', waiting to follow.

When he came out of the hotel, it was not by the main entrance at the corner but through the café entrance at the side. He did not walk toward his car at all. He came straight across the street, straight toward us, as though he knew we were waiting.

There was no way out. He would hear us if we hurried out the back way, over the trash and broken branches. He would see us if we went out to the street. There was a drainspout and a bit of a false front at the edge of the hardware store. Alex, Dickie and Linda hugged the shadows along the sandstone wall. Sam and I huddled across from them against the old caragana bush at the corner of Paulins'. I have never since known whether the thrill I felt was because of the warmth of Sam's body in close against mine or because of the danger of the man crossing the street toward us. All I know is I must have used up every bit of adrenalin in my body during the thirty seconds or so it took him to cross the street.

Then he walked right past us. Even though it had been closed since five thirty, someone let him into Paulins' store. We waited.

"What if he was hired to kill Mr. Paulins?" Alex asked in a whisper.

We just looked at him. Alex always had to have his "what if." I had my doubts. After all, Mr. Paulins had let him in the store. At least, someone had, and who else would be in the store at eight o'clock at night?

"What," he continued, "if he sneaks out the back door after?"

Just to be sure, we sent Dickie and Linda to watch the back exit to the store. There was no telling what a hired gun might do.

What he did was leave by the front door, right behind Mr. Paulins. The briefcase had apparently been left behind. They crossed the street and walked down the alley behind the Crown, parallel to First Avenue. At a good safe distance behind them, we followed. Thinking back on it now, it's amazing that they never noticed, lurking in the shadows behind them, five kids with bikes.

They stuck to the alleys for two blocks, crossing Second Street west and continuing up the alley behind the Rialto. Then, still keeping to the shadows, they turned right and followed Third Street to First Avenue. They crossed quickly, walking along the side of the Co-op Store to the alley, then turning right quickly into the darkness behind the store.

"What do we do now?" Dickie whispered.

"Follow," I said.

"Split up," Alex added.

"Good," I said, "you guys go down between the Chinaman's and the Co-op. Sam and I will take the street side. But be careful."

"Why do you get the street?" asked Alex.

"Because I beat you to the draw," I said.

He nodded, and we split into two groups to trail after Mr. Paulins and the stranger.

Staying out of sight behind the Co-op was never any problem. There were large garbage bins and stacked wooden cases for pop and piles of cardboard cartons waiting for the garbage pick-up. Sam and I leaned our bikes on the side of the building and crept around back, not on our hands and knees of course, but the sense was the same. From the shadows, we could see the two men standing near the rear entrance of the store. The other man was watching as Mr. Paulins pointed out something on the door. They were speaking very softly, so that we could not hear what was said between them.

Across from us, among the cardboard cartons, we could see Dickie, so we knew the others must be there too.

"What are you up to!" The voice came from the alley behind the other kids. It sounded familiar to me, that gruff quality, but I was too scared at the time to place it.

Mr. Paulins and the stranger rushed quietly past where Sam and I were hidden and back the way they had come. We picked up our bikes and followed.

Alex and Linda caught up to us by the Rialto. Dickie was not with them. We had agreed to meet back at the Crown if we got separated, so the four of us waited there. When the café closed at ten, Dickie had not yet shown.

We never again saw Dickie alive.

From the shadows we could see the two men standing near the rear entrance of the store. The other man was watching as Mr. Paulins pointed out something on the door. They were speaking very softly, so that we could not hear what was said between them.

Chapter 7

Dickie had been missing three days before he was found. He was lying in the old gravel pit, down at the bottom near the slough of stagnant water that collects there, as though asleep. Mrs. Ryerson and Susan had taken their setter out to give him a swim and a run. While her mother got old Red out of the station wagon, Susan walked over to the water. She could not have missed him had she wanted to, lying face down on the gravel like that. It took poor Susan years to get over that find. I think it took the four of us as long, if we are over it yet.

We had been with him, or rather he had been with us, that night behind the Co-op Store, the night he had disappeared. Alex and I especially felt at fault; we had asked the others to help us follow the stranger.

There was no inquest. Dr. Lyman, the town doctor, gave Dickie a looking over, but that was about it. He was badly banged up, especially around the right temple. Dr. Lyman said Dickie had obviously fallen from the edge of the gravel pit, battering himself against the rocks and roots on the way down, then attempted to crawl toward the water. The water would not have revived him, said Dr. Lyman. The Mounties agreed. It was a death by misadventure, an accident.

It was a misadventure. We agreed, but it was no accident. Tom Porter had not believed us about the stranger, about his gun, so we did not tell him about that night behind the Co-op. Why would he believe us, a bunch of kids, when everyone knew how Dickie had died?

Dickie was buried Monday afternoon in the old town cemetery. Nearly everyone in town was there. That's how it is in a small town when a kid dies. The whole community shares the pain with the family.

The stranger was not there, of course, and neither was Mr. Dutka, who had come to Elizabeth from Edmonton to manage the Co-op Store and had always been somewhat of an outsider, nor were Mr. Sweeney and the few other loners we had in town. There were a lot of people at that funeral and nearly every business in town had closed for the afternoon.

That night we did not follow the stranger. We had not gone near him since Dickie had disappeared. Still, none of us had the heart to stay home alone with our thoughts. After supper, without really having planned it, we met at the Crown.

We had been talking about the songs on the jukebox, about school just over, about other kids, about anything that would avoid what was on all our minds.

Alex had been sitting quietly, picking at his plate of chips. The subject would not be avoided.

"He did it," Alex said.

"Alex, don't," Linda said softly, as though not wanting to hear herself, let alone Alex. Alex was not about to be stopped.

"That man killed Dickie. That hired gun."

"I don't know," I said.

"He did it. And all we can do is sit here feeling sorry for ourselves."

"That's not true," Sam said, not entirely with conviction.

"Fact," said Alex, "plain, simple fact."

"Maybe it wasn't him," I said.

"You heard him, Bobby. He saw us."

"I heard someone. Behind you. He was in front, with Mr. Paulins."

"That's right," said Sam, "I heard the voice too. He was somewhere behind you."

"And your hired gun took off with Mr. Paulins. We followed," I added.

It was the first time since that night we had dared talk about what had happened. Alex looked like he did not believe us.

"Linda?"

"I don't know, Alex. It was dark, and I was scared. It may have been the stranger. It may not have been. I really don't know."

"Alex, it was someone else."

"Who then, Bobby? Who?"

"I don't know. At the time there was something about the voice. I knew the voice, Alex."

"Who was it, Bobby?"

"I don't know. I've been trying since Wednesday, but I can't quite make out what it was about that voice. For sure it was not Mr. Paulins or that other guy though. For sure."

Sam nodded her head in agreement.

It was hard for any of us to accept. Before Wednesday, Alex and I had worried that the hired gun might have recognized us at the dump, that he might kill us. Now, if we were to accept what Sam and I had heard, somewhere in town there must be another killer.

The jukebox had run out, but none of us heard the silence. Usually, one of us would have jumped up, plunked a few coins in the box, and selected a dozen or so songs. We sat, doing nothing, saying nothing.

I am not sure, except in a general sense, what the others were thinking. In my mind, over and over, I was hearing a voice I somehow recognized:

"What are you up to!"

A voice heard from the dark shadows of a back alley, the voice of a killer. There was something about that voice, but try as I might I could not place it.

Chapter 8

After the funeral, the talk of the town was again the Co-op Store scandal. There was a rumour that an auditor was to be brought in from Edmonton to go over the store's books, and that the RCMP might even bring in a special team of investigators.

According to The Gazette, Mr. Dutka had at first dismissed the whole thing as a bunch of rumours. Later, after being pressured by James Wyatt and Tom Porter to do a quick audit, Mr. Dutka had admitted that there might be a few shortages at his store.

While The Gazette played the story down, the gossips converted those admitted few shortages into hundreds and perhaps thousands of dollars in merchandise and cash. The skitterish members of the Elizabeth Farmer's Co-operative (U.F.A.) began to pressure their Board of Directors to hire a new manager for the store. The Board waited to see the report from the auditor, whom they had in fact sent for.

Most of this we heard second hand, through overheard conversations around town and at home, or through stories in The Gazette. Our own concerns were more immediate. Someone in town had killed Dickie, and any one of us might be his next victim. We tried for a couple more days to pretend nothing had happened. I don't think any of us slept well during that time, if at all.

Thursday night at the Crown, Sam had had enough. All of us had, I suppose, but it was Sam who again brought the subject into our conversation.

"Bobby, we've got to do something."

"A movie?" I tried to pretend I had misunderstood her. She would have none of that.

"I'm serious. We can't just sit here and wait for him to kill us all."

"So what do we do?" I asked.

"Yeah, what?" Alex followed.

"Find the killer."

Linda had sat silently through all this. Now I heard her breath in sharply. Alex beat me to the question.

"How?"

"Well, by following people I guess."

"After what happened?" I asked.

"Especially after what happened. What else have we got?"

"Sam's right, Bobby. Maybe if we follow Mr. Black Lincoln we can find out something," said Alex.

"And Mr. Paulins. We should see what he's up to too," added Sam.

I was worried. I thought again of that voice I had almost recognized in the dark. Sam seemed to read my thoughts as she watched me from across the booth.
"Maybe you'll remember."
"What?"
"That voice in the alley. Maybe you'll remember who it is, Bobby."
"Yeah, maybe."
Since the hotel and Mr. Paulins' grocery store were across the street from each other, we could watch both from our vantage in the Crown café. We agreed that Alex and Linda
would follow the stranger if he left the hotel. Sam and I would follow Mr. Paulins if he left the store.
The next morning we renewed our surveillance.

Chapter 9

For two days, all was quiet. Except for his nightly trips to the dump for target practice, the hired gun stayed at the hotel or went out for meals. He did nothing unusual that we noticed. Mr. Paulins stayed in his store most of the day, except for the bank deposit at six each night, and stayed in his apartment above the store all night.

Saturday night, just before closing, the stranger came out of the hotel by the side entrance and crossed the street to Paulins' Store. Through the window we could see him walk directly to the counter, where Mr. Paulins was making up his deposit. They spoke calmly at first, then the conversation seemed to become more heated. It ended with Mr. Paulins shaking his head and gesturing with his hands as though he were very emphatically saying no. The other man turned and walked toward the door. We scattered and hid.

When the stranger had returned to the hotel, Alex and Linda went back to the café. Sam and I watched

Mr. Paulins through the window for a while longer. He had picked up the telephone as soon as the stranger left. As he spoke on the telephone, he seemed angry. He slammed the receiver down. As he walked over to lock up, we rushed across the street to join the others at the Crown.

Half an hour later, Mr. Paulins turned off the lights in the store and walked out the front door, locking it behind him. He walked straight across the street and down the alley behind the hotel. Sam and I picked up our bikes from the rack outside, then followed.

The route was the same as we had taken before, through the alleys, past the Rialto, and down Third Street to the back of the Co-op Store. By the time we had leaned our bikes against the side of the store and crept to where we could watch from behind a garbage bin, Mr. Paulins had given the back door of the Co-op several loud raps. Then he waited, his feet shuffling against the concrete stoop.

Sam put her hand in mine. I squeezed. Somehow it helped. The terror of being here, in this exact spot again, became less with the warmth of her hand.

The iron door creaked and a block of light burst into the dark around Mr. Paulins. In this new light, Mr. Paulins looked faded and ghostly, but more than that he looked terribly afraid. A distorted shadow against the stacked cardboard boxes across from us beckoned. Mr. Paulins followed the man who had made the shadow, and the door closed behind them.

I began to move toward the door. Sam's hand squeezed mine tightly.

Sam and I watched Mr. Paulins through the window for a while longer. He had picked up the telephone as soon as the stranger left. As he spoke on the telephone, he seemed angry. He slammed the receiver down.

"Come on," I said, "let's see what we can hear."

There was a slight hesitation, then she followed. Neither of us said anything more.   The door was shut tightly, and it was too solid to allow any sounds out of the Co-op. I looked around. About ten feet up the wall was a row of small windows. One was open. Below it was a stack of wooden pop cases.

"Keep watch," I whispered. Sam nodded and I let go her hand.

Sam stood below while I climbed the steps created by the stack of wooden boxes. When I reached the top I carefully looked in the open window. It was a small office, but there was nobody in it. From beyond the open office door I could hear voices, but they were too far to be clear. The words were not understandable, but the mood was: these were angry men.

The voices moved further away, and I hurried to get back to Sam below. We had just gotten behind the pop cases when the steel door opened again and Mr. Paulins walked out.

"You're asking too much," I heard him say.

The voice from inside was cold. If the words were not a threat, the tone most assuredly was.

"You'll handle it."

Mr. Paulins said nothing. He just walked away, back the way he had come.

"Handle it," said the voice, and the light disappeared as the door closed.

My whole body was cold. There was no mistaking the voice of the man we had not seen.

"Sam?"

"You want to follow him?"
"Sam, it's him."
"Who?"
"The man in the store. He's the one who got Dickie.
It's the same voice."
"For sure?"
"For sure."
"Who is it?"
"I don't know. Not really."
"Should we follow Mr. Paulins?"
"No. Let's wait."
We crouched behind those pop cases, watching the lights in the windows above for more than fifteen minutes. When the lights finally went out, we watched the back door of the Co-op. Nobody came out.

We heard a car starting at the front of the store. By the time we got to the front, all we could see was taillights of a car turning from First Avenue left onto Main Street. From that distance, it looked like maybe a new Custom Royal, but I could not tell for sure. It may or may not have been the one we had heard.

I took Sam's hand and we walked back to the Crown to tell Alex and Linda what we had learned. The man who had killed Dickie had keys to the Co-op Store. Alex and Linda told us that the stranger had not moved from the hotel all night. They had seen Mr. Paulins let himself back into the store about twenty minutes before we had returned. Now the lights of his apartment upstairs were turned off.

We went home.

Chapter 10

I had a lot of trouble sleeping that night. Life had become very complicated, and I had not even reached my thirteenth birthday. There were two killers in town, and both could be after me and my friends. I lay back on my bed watching the curtains drifting gently inward and back to the wall on the breeze from my upstairs window. It was a clear, quiet night. I could see the white disc of the moon, sharp as a harrow disc against the deep blue field of the sky. The night insects sang their trilling songs, punctuated by the occasional chortle of a frog and in the distance somewhere the howl of a coyote or dog.

Sometime very late I heard the two sharp reports, like firecrackers set off in the night. It sounded like they were up around main street, about a block away. They could have been set off somewhere near Paulins' Store or the Crown Hotel. It was hard to tell exactly.

Looking out my window across the wide vacant lot of our apartment building I could see the back of Paulins'

I had a lot of trouble sleeping that night. Life had become very complicated, and I had not even reached my thirteenth birthday. There were two killers in town, and both could be after me and my friends.

and through the spaces between the buildings the hotel beyond. There was not a living soul in sight.

Back in my bed, I watched the moon watching me until I at last fell asleep.

My mother must have known I had been awake late, because she went to work without waking me. It was past ten when I got up. I dressed quickly and hurried to the Crown. The others were already there.

"What happened to you?" asked Alex.

"Slept in."

I sat down. Nobody said anything.

"What's with you guys?"

They took a while to answer. When Sam finally spoke, I was sorry I had asked.

"It's Mr. Paulins. He shot himself last night. He was found early this morning at his kitchen table, dead."

What was I to say?

The very morning after Mr. Paulins was found slumped over his kitchen table shot dead, the stranger left town.

"I told you so," said Alex.

"Sure," I said. We were in the boiler room of the apartment building, loading the coal hopper that fed the furnace that heated the boilers for the building's steam heat. I had never understood why this needed doing in the summer, but for a few dollars spending money I was willing to shovel a bit of coal. Carrying a shovel full of black nuggets from the coal bin to the hopper, I was in no mood for long conversations. Outside it was ninety degrees. I hoisted the shovel and dumped its contents into the hopper.

"I mean it," Alex said as he shoved his shovel deep into the black mountain, "He's a hired gun. Someone hired him to get Mr. Paulins." He lifted the full shovel and began walking back toward the hopper.

"Why?" I said, taking my turn at the coal bin.

"Who knows," he grunted as he heaved the coal into the hopper, "but the job's done and the killer's gone."

I hoisted my now full shovel and turned to face him.

"Too many westerns. That's your problem, you've been watching too many westerns."

"Yeah? Then who did it, Bobby?"

"Easy." My shovel full of coal crashed into the growing pile in the hopper. "Mr. Paulins. Suicide."

"I tell you Bobby, it was the hired gun. It was him. That's why he's gone now." Alex had stopped shovelling and stood leaning on his shovel. "His job is finished."

"His job," we had been feeling almost elated that the man had gone, feeling safe, "Alex, what about the other one?"

"What other?"

The hopper growled ominously as it shifted another dose of coal into the old furnace. The fire roared.

"Whoever killed Dickie, Alex."

We stood silently in the half light of the boiler room, the only sounds the soft rush of the fire and a songbird somewhere in the distance outside.

Suddenly Alex turned and rammed his shovel deep into the coal pile, lifting his overfull load and heaving it

into the hopper. I followed. In no time we had our job
done and were back outside in the fresh summer air.

Chapter 11

The tension in Elizabeth was almost visible, like the slender waves of heat that rose like grass from the ground distorting all in sight. The auditors that had at first been rumoured and then promised had not yet arrived. Members of the Co-op wanted answers. They had heard thousands of dollars in cash and merchandise were missing from the store. The Board of Directors was being pressured from every direction to do something about it. Everyone who worked at the Co-op bore a cloud of suspicion, and most of all Mr. Dutka, the manager. Mr. Dutka had always been a flashy dresser and he had only recently bought a brand new three-tone Custom Royal. Besides, he was not one of us; he had come to Elizabeth from the city. He was an outsider. There's no telling what an outsider might do. That was the talk around town.

Our talk was of other matters. As far as we knew, there was still a killer loose in town. If there was, then he might come after any one of us. After all, we had been with Dickie just before he disappeared. We sat at the Crown and tried to sort the whole thing out.

"Alex," I said, "what if you're right about Mr. Paulins not killing himself?"

"I'm right. Listen, there were two shots. You said you heard them yourself, two. How does a man who has just shot himself to death fire that second shot, eh?"

"My dad says Dr. Lyman figures it was the nerves. He says the fingers just tightened up when the first bullet hit the brain and fired the second shot. Automatic."

"That's crazy!"

"It's what Dr. Lyman says. He says with a pistol like that it's easy. Happens lots of times."

"Sure."

"Anyway, if someone did kill him, what if it wasn't the stranger?"

"No!" Linda said it softly, but we all looked her way. Her eyes were large, like they would pop out. Alex put his hand on her shoulder.

"The man at the Co-op?" said Sam. I suppose we had all been thinking it. The hard thing was to face it, but it had to be faced.

I just nodded.

"Two nothing," said Alex.

"What?" I asked.

"The score. Zero for the hired gun; two for the mystery man."

"That's horrible," said Sam.

"But true," said Alex.

The silence between us was so deep even the jukebox was not able to penetrate it. It was as though we had entered a tomb. A whispered voice broke the spell.

"We're next," said Linda, so low we hardly heard her.

"We've got to stop him," I said.

"How?" asked Alex. "Who do we stop?"

Who? That was the problem. None of us had any idea who the killer was. How would we stop an evil we did not know? How could we discover and expose this killer before he could get to us?

"Let's talk to Tom," suggested Sam.

"He won't believe us," said Alex.

"Maybe he will."

"He didn't believe about the hired gun. Why would he believe this?"

"Why don't we just try him?"

"It's worth a try," I said.

"If he doesn't believe us, we've lost nothing," added Linda.

"Yeah, okay," said Alex.

"Let's go find him now," said Sam. So we all got up and went looking for the Mountie. He patrolled the town on no
set schedule, so we got on our bikes and cruised the streets until we found him out in the new subdivision.

"Come on. I'll buy you all a Coke," Tom said, after we told him we wanted to talk to him, and we all trooped back to the Chinaman's. Tom was like that, always good with the kids, willing to spend a bit of time with us. That did not mean that he would believe us. I don't think even Sam really thought he would believe our story.

"Tom, we think there is a killer in town," Sam started.

"Is this about that gun again?" he asked, looking pointedly at Alex.

"No," I said. Sam continued.

"We think someone killed Dickie Simmons. On purpose. The same man, he might have killed Mr. Paulins too."

"The man at the hotel. The man Alex says has a gun. Right?" asked Tom.

"No, sir. Someone else entirely," said Sam.

"Someone at the Co-op," I added.

"What? Are you kids pulling my leg?"

"It's true," said Alex, and Linda nodded in agreement.

"Where do you kids come up with these stories?" Tom was definitely beginning to doubt our story. We were going to have a real job of it making him believe. That was for sure.

"We saw him!" said Alex.

"Saw who?" asked Tom.

"The killer," Alex clarified.

"No," I said. "Not really."

"What's this all about, Bobby?" I don't know why Tom asked me. At the time, I supposed it was because Alex tended so often to exaggerate and the others were, after all, just girls.

"Let's go find him now," said Sam. So we all got up and went looking for the Mountie. He patrolled the town on no set schedule, so we got on our bikes and cruised the streets until we found him out in the new subdivision.

"We didn't tell you before. We thought you wouldn't believe us. The night Dickie disappeared, we followed the stranger and Mr. Paulins."

"Uh huh," he said. I went on.

"They walked to the Co-op and went around back. Mr. Paulins was showing the stranger something. I don't know what, but it was near the back door."

"Tell him about the money," said Alex.

"Oh yeah, when the stranger came to town we saw him put a big pile of money in the Treasury Branch. That night he took a whole bunch out and put it in a briefcase. He left the briefcase at Mr. Paulins' before they went together to the Co-op."

"And before that, we saw them arguing about something."

"So then, Alex, you're saying the stranger killed Mr. Paulins?"

"No," I answered for Alex, "It's just funny, that's all, the way the stranger gave Mr. Paulins all that money then Mr. Paulins showed him something at the Co-op."

"Then what are you saying?"

"Well, let me finish."

"Go on."

"So there we were, the five of us, watching the stranger and Mr. Paulins. Suddenly, behind Dickie and Alex and Linda, somebody yelled. We all took off, even the two men. We never saw Dickie again. Not until the funeral."

"And you think...?"

"Whoever yelled killed Dickie," said Alex.

"And his voice sounded awful familiar to me," I added.

"Who was it?"

"I don't know, Tom. I keep trying to remember."

"About Mr. Paulins," Sam kept the story going, "We followed him to the Co-op alone. He met someone."

"It was the same voice," I said, "They argued."

"That was the night Mr. Paulins died," Tom guessed.

"Yes," I said.

"And you have never seen this man, only heard his voice?"

I nodded.

"All right, say I believe you. What am I to do with this?"

We just looked at him.

"Look at it from my point of view. What do I report back to Mountbatten. That I have four twelve year olds who say one accidental death and one suicide were both murders? That the same twelve year olds imagine they might recognize the voice of the killer, but that they have never seen him? That there is no other evidence of wrongdoing, and no motive?"

He paused, but only briefly.

"If you were my bosses, what would you say."

"I wouldn't believe it," I said.

"Right," said Tom.

"Does that mean you don't believe us?" asked Sam.

"No. I believe you. I can't tell you why. But we have no proof. Let me poke around a bit. And you kids stay out of it, you hear."

We all nodded agreement. I don't think any of us really meant it.

We thanked Tom for the Cokes and left him alone in the booth. Mr. Dutka walked in as we walked out. He was a big man with a handlebar mustache, who looked crammed into his expensive city suit. Not the sort you would want to run into in a dark alley. As we walked past the big front window of the Chinaman's, I saw him join Tom Porter in his booth.

I supposed they were going to discuss the problems at the Co-op Store, the disappearances of thousands of dollars worth of cash and merchandise. Mr. Dutka had some serious problems.

The disappearances from the Co-op. That brought me back to Dickie. He too had disappeared from the Co-op Store. Something was nagging at the back of my mind, something powerful enough that I do not remember at all our walk back that day from the Chinaman's to the Crown.

Chapter 12

"It's the car," I said.
"It's alive, it speaks," said Alex.
We were sitting at the Crown.
"Hush, Alex," said Sam.
"The car, a Custom Royal. That's pretty fancy."
"What's it about, Bobby?" asked Sam.
"The car. Remember, Sam? The night Mr. Paulins died, we saw a car driving away. I forgot to tell Tom about that."
"Don't believe us anyway," Alex cut in.
"What about the car?" asked Sam.
"Custom Royal. I'm sure of it, the car I saw was a Custom Royal. New One."
"Big deal," said Alex, "who owns a fancy car like that around here?"
"Mr. Dutka," said Linda.
"Mr. Dutka," I agreed.
"What's that supposed to mean?" asked Alex.

"Maybe it was Mr. Dutka who took off like a bat out of hell that night. Maybe it was his car I saw turning onto Main Street that night."

"Important man like him? He ain't gonna kill anyone," said Alex.

"Maybe," I said.

"There's been a lot taken from the Co-op," said Sam, "maybe by Mr. Dutka."

"Maybe," I said. I was not sure I wanted to admit it.

"Mr. Paulins and him were arguing at the reservoir," said Linda. I had forgotten about that.

"How can we prove it," Alex asked.

"I don't know," I said.

"Follow him," said Sam.

It seemed the only way. After a lot of discussion, we went along with Sam. That night we would follow Mr. Dutka. We would follow him every night until we could find out what he was up to, until we could prove he had killed our friend.

Each night we waited, Sam and I behind the pop cases at the back of the Co-op watching the back door, Alex and Linda across First Avenue watching the front door. Each night Mr. Dutka walked out the front door, got into his new Custom Royal, and drove home. We began to wonder if we had got caught up in our parents' paranoia about the thefts at the Co-op and our killer was not Mr. Dutka at all.

Chapter 13

About five days after he had left, the man we had all taken to calling the hired gun returned to town. We were all sitting at our usual table near the jukebox when his black Lincoln pulled up outside the Crown.

"What's he back for?" wondered Alex.

The rest of us sat silently, watching the stranger in his dark city clothes walking toward the main entrance of the hotel.

"Us," Alex decided out loud, "Unfinished business. He's come back for us."

"Come on, Alex," I said.

"We'll have to watch him," said Sam, and we all knew she was right. Right there and then we decided to split up. This time Sam and I would watch the stranger while Alex and Linda watched Mr. Dutka, even though by now we had figured he was innocent.

Over the next few days, not much happened. As he had in the past, the stranger spent his days quietly, walking around town or staying at the hotel, always seeming to see everything that went on around him. In the evening he would drive to the dump for an hour of target practice, then go back to his room at the hotel and stay there. Mr. Dutka drove straight home from work each night.

Tom Porter had told us nothing new and we had learned nothing on our own. We began to think nothing would happen, ever. We met at the Crown and decided to give it until the end of the week, Saturday night, and then give up. That was Thursday.

Friday, the stranger stayed in his room all day. When it came time for target practice, he still stayed in his room. When Alex and Linda came back to the Crown after watching Mr. Dutka drive away from the Co-op, he was still in his room.

At about nine o'clock, the stranger walked into the café, right past us and out the side entrance of the hotel. We followed him. He took the by now familiar route through the alleys and down past the Rialto to the Co-op Store. We stayed about a block behind. After all, as soon as he turned into the alley behind the hotel we knew where he was going.

We were halfway across First Avenue when I saw it, the car.

"He's there!"

"Who?" asked Sam.

"Mr. Dutka."

"You're crazy," said Alex.

"No. There in front, that's his car. The Custom Royal."

"He's right," said Sam.

We all went down the sidewalk side of the Co-op. After the night Dickie disappeared, none of us wanted to chance the other side. When we came around to the alley, the back door was partly open, sending a shaft of light into the darkness. The stranger was there, fallen and still on the ground in front of that open door.

We saw nobody else around.

Slowly, I walked over to the slumped form of the man we had been following. The others followed. I bent and felt the man's neck. I had seen that done on television. I felt him breathing, felt his heartbeat in the arteries. On the side of his head was a small cut at the centre of a large red mark.

"Someone's hit him. He's alive," I said.

Before anyone else could answer, someone spoke out of the darkness behind us.

"Not for long. Sorry kids. Into the store, now! You boys, you drag him in. And no tricks."

The voice was gruff, harsh, familiar.

"It's him!" I said.

"Yes," said Sam.

"Shut up and move it!" said the voice behind us.

Alex and I started to drag the stranger's body over the threshold and into the Co-op Store. The girls stepped in behind us. I looked up just as the man stepped into the light. Mr. Dutka pointed the stranger's gun straight at me.

"Move," he said.

We did. We pulled the stranger into the store and Mr. Dutka walked in behind us. Keeping his eyes on

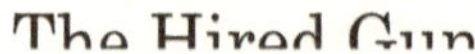

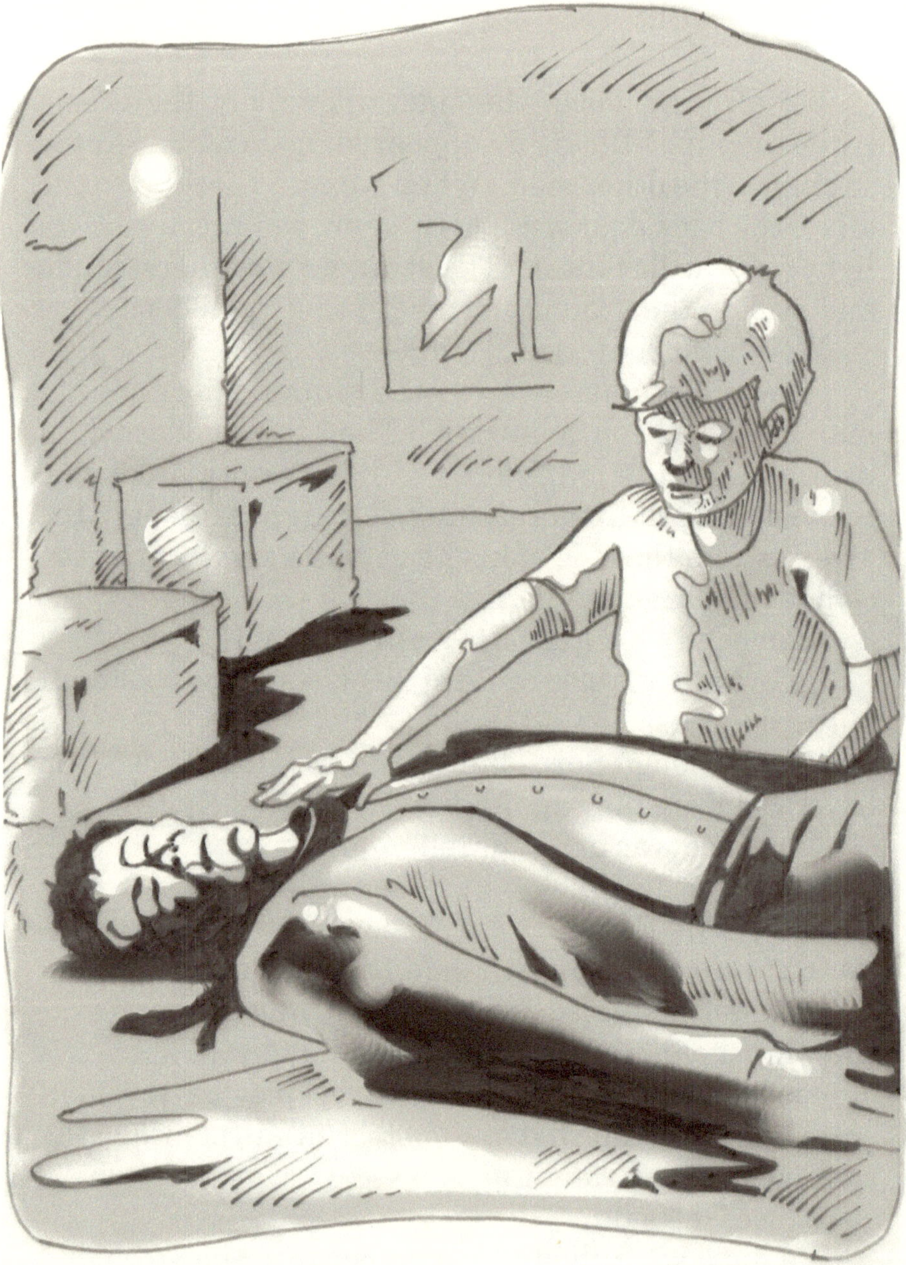

I bent and felt the man's neck. I had seen that done on television. I felt him breathing, felt his heartbeat in the arteries. On the side of his head was a small cut at the centre of a large red mark. "Someone's hit him. He's alive," I said.

us, the gun in his right hand pointed straight at me, he reached back with his left to pull the door closed.

His whole body snapped back as another hand, reaching from outside, pulled back hard. The gun snapped upward, putting a couple of bullets into the ceiling. Alex and I both had the same thought. We rushed forward, butting Mr. Dutka in the stomach with our heads and hands. He flew back into the doorframe, smashing his head and sliding downward in a slumped heap.

The door opened fully. In walked Tom Porter, followed by two Mounties I had never seen before.

"I thought I told you kids to stay out of this," he said.

"Yes, Sir," Alex and I said in unison. The girls were silent. Behind me I heard the stranger starting to get up.

"Look out!" I cried as I spun around.

Tom laughed as I propelled myself at the half-sitting man and we both fell to the floor in a heap.

"Bobby," said Tom, "I'd like to introduce you to Inspector Hogan. He has been investigating Mr. Dutka for embezzlement and, more recently, for the murders of your friend Dickie Simmons and of Mr. Paulins."

Sam had come up to me and gave me her hand to help me up. I stood, but I did not let go of her hand. It felt good to be with her at a time like this. It felt good to have someone. After all, Alex was just a guy.

That was the summer we all grew up. And that was how we learned the truth about the man Alex had called the hired gun.

Bob MacKenzie

Bob MacKenzie has published a dozen books of poetry and prose-fiction and his work has been featured in numerous anthologies. His arts reviews and commentary have been published in many newspapers, on CBC radio, in academic journals, and online. His writing has also been published as prestigious numbered limited-edition hand-made letterpress art-books by *The Brandstead Press* and *Thee Hellbox Press*. Bob's novels *Ghost Shadow: Unfinished Sins* and *Another Eternity* and his poetry collection *On Edge* have all been winners of international awards and he has received an Ontario Arts Council grant for literature and a Canada Council grant to support his performance. Bob's poetry has appeared in hundreds of magazines, journals, and anthologies internationally. Many of his poems have been reproduced by visual artists and sculptors and a public art gallery has devoted an entire visual arts exhibition to his poetry. He is possibly the only poet to have versions of his poetry owned by the Canada Council's National Art Bank. Both on his own and with the performance ensemble Poem de Terre, Bob has performed much of his poetry live with original music. Six albums of Bob's spoken performances with Poem de Terre have been released.

Mike St. Pierre

Illustrator Mike St. Pierre's career as an artist got an early start. Born in 1958, Mike began drawing in early childhood and, by the age of 15, had sold many oil paintings throughout Ontario. Many of Mike's pieces now hang in private collections and in the Hockey Hall of Fame. In 1980, Mike graduated from St, Lawrence College in Kingston, Ontario, with a diploma for Fine Arts. He went on in 1981 to become Art Director of the Cataraqui Conservation Authority, then freelanced for advertising agencies in Toronto and Ottawa for several years doing magazine illustration and record albums, CD covers, and book covers. Mike is experienced in all aspects of illustration and airbrush work and he now runs a popular freelance airbrushing and illustration service in Eastern Ontario.

The Dugout

a short story

Bob MacKenzie

cover photo: public domain (google search)

The Dugout

The year I was sixteen old man Hawkins died and Tommy and I found the human bones on his property. It was 1966 and old man Hawkins had been living on that big farm at the edge of town for almost exactly fifty years. Although he had never been much for associating with people, over time he became one of Elizabeth's leading citizens. I suppose his money had a lot to do with that.

In 1905 Alberta had become a province of Canada. Elizabeth was already a town of some 300 souls. A year later, Galen Hawkins registered his claim to one hundred acres of scrub covered rolling hills just outside town. He loaded his wagon with enough supplies to hold him that summer and all the next winter, then he rode alone to his new property. That was all anyone saw of Galen Hawkins until the next spring.

He had grown a beard, and he was thinner, so people were not sure who the stranger might be until he walked into Walling's General Store, announcing quietly, "I'm Galen Hawkins, from over east of town. I'll be needing some supplies."

Most folks out here were dirt poor back then. Nobody knew where this Hawkins came from, so when he paid cash they just assumed he must have come from the east rich. After that, whenever he came to town he paid cash. Right up to the day he died.

Anyway, I always had an interest in local history, even when I was a kid, so I looked up just about everybody. The little snoop, some people called me. When it came to Galen Hawkins, about all I ever found out from town records and the newspaper was that he came to town, paid cash, and never really had to farm for a living. Local legend, though, had it that he was the very man who had shot down the notorious Isobel Simms. Of course, I never put much stock in that.

When I say he never had to farm what I mean is that he ran a few cattle and some horses, but they ran pretty wild. He never tried to market his livestock and he never put in crops. About all he did to improve the land was to put up that big eastern style gingerbread house with a bunkhouse attached and a barn beside it.

He did, of course, put up the fences. They were barbed and electric both. He said it was to keep the animals in, but the signs told everyone it was also to keep us out. He had dogs, near wild shepherds, and outsiders hired as guards to patrol the fence. He called them hired hands, but they had guns, all of them, and never associated with us in town.

Even as young as ten or twelve, we would ride our bikes out to the Hawkins place and look for ways to get in. For young boys there was nothing quite as challenging as to enter the secret empire of Galen

Hawkins. He was a man of mystery and his land a fortress to be stormed.

Barbed wire and electric fences are no real problem for the enterprising boy. There were places at the back and sides of the property where trees had been cut down to make the fence line more clear. A kid could stand on a stump, place one foot atop a wooden fence post, and jump across the wire hazard. In other places, erosion or animals had lowered the earth below the fence enough so that a kid could use a forked stick to raise the wire, then slip under.

Tommy and I were in and out of the Hawkins property quite often, but we never went too far for fear of the guards. We wanted to be sure we could get out again. So, except for a narrow strip around the edges farthest from that big white house, most of Hawkins' land remained a mystery to us. I suppose that is why we were so eager to go in when he died.

I was probably one of the first to hear. I was in the Gazette office reading up on Luke Barfield.

Luke Barfield was a kind of local hero with us kids. Between 1899 and 1906, he had engineered a series of train and bank robberies in Alberta and Montana that must surely have made him one of the richest men in the Territories.

What thrilled our young minds was that only two people, Luke and a notoriously beautiful lady named Isobel Simms, performed the robberies, and they vanished as though by magic after each robbery. No one was ever able to learn where.

The closest they came to getting caught was in November of 1906, when the Alberta Provincial Police happened upon a Royal Mail train just as it was being robbed. Although they had never shot anyone, Luke had always intimidated their victims with his American Colt 45 pistol. Rather than take chances, the police fired, killing Isobel Simms. And Luke Barfield only barely escaped with his life. He was never seen again. Police believed he had been hit bad and died somewhere in the hills.

But I am wandering. As I said, I was there in the Gazette office when Rudy Gollens, one of old man Hawkins' hired hands came in.

"You seen Doc Fletcher?" he asked Mr. Edson, who was working at his typewriter.

"Not in his office?"

"No."

"Haven't seen him. You see him, Bobby?"

I had thought of myself as invisible, sitting there listening. Obviously I was not.

"No. Not for a while," I answered.

"What's up?" asked Mr. Edson.

"Old man died last night. Heart, I think. Want Doc to take a look at him," said Rudy.

"I see him, I'll send him on out. You been to Lyall's yet?"

"I'll be going there now."

Lyall's was the funeral home in Elizabeth, still is for that matter. I had heard enough. I replaced the scrapbook I had been reading and went to find Tommy.

***

"This is crazy, Bobby. We shouldn't be here."

"It's the best time. The guards will all be in town at the funeral. The dogs are locked up. Come on."

"I don't know."

"Hey, Tommy. We're here now."

We had ridden our bikes out to the north east corner of the Hawkins property and had used an old stump to help us cross the fence. Now we were about twenty yards inside the fence. Tommy hesitated for a moment more, then shrugged.

"Well, okay."

We walked through the woods and came out in back of that big old house. As I had thought, there was nobody around and the dogs were in their wire pens.

"Come on," I said, and started walking across the barnyard toward the house. Tommy was slow, but he followed. The back door was open.

The house was very much what you would expect a rich man's farm house to be. The furniture was about as old as the house, but well kept, all rich, dark woods and thick upholstery. There were nicknacks and fine porcelain and beautiful old lamps. There were paintings throughout the house, but there was only one photograph.

"Let's get out of here. It's spooky."

"Okay, Tommy," I said, but I could not resist taking one souvenir. We hurried down the stairs and back out the back door the way we came. It was on the way back to our bikes that we stumbled on the dugout, an old sod house half in a hillside and half out, now all collapsed so it seemed just another irregularity of the land.

We were running through a clearing in the poplars when Tommy stumbled. I went back to help him and I saw it.

"A board!"

"What?"

"It's a board. Tommy, you tripped over a regular man made board. What's a board doing out here?"

"Who knows? Who cares? Let's get out of here."

"Let's look first."

Near the board was an opening in the earth about two feet by two feet. Around it I could see other boards, broken and sticking from the earth, and I could see in this hump on the earth the bare shape of what must have been a building about ten feet square.

"It's a dugout," I said.

"A what?"

"A house. A pioneer house."

"Oh. Can we go now?" Tommy knew better than to ask, but he did anyway.

"Looks like the beams have held. Let's go in." I figured the hole was big enough to crawl through. I went in feet first. Tommy waited outside. The wine smell of damp rotted wood and the muskier odour of damp earth filled the dark interior of the dugout. All I could see was a narrow area lit by the shaft of light from the opening I had come in by.

"Hey, Tommy. You got matches?"

"Lighter, why?"

"Give me it, and a piece of that paper you're always carrying around."

I lit the paper he handed me and looked around the small room. It was sparsely furnished, as I suppose the home of a homesteader must have been fifty years ago. I had been poking around for a few minutes when my eye was caught by something white reflecting my makeshift torch from a far corner. It was a sort of silver pendant, a medal I suppose, or a badge. On it was inscribed the words, "Alberta Provincial Police." It was hung by a silver chain around the neck of a crumpled skeleton, the head of which was shattered. By impulse more than design I reached out and turned over the bright metal. On the back was engraved, "Galen Hawkins, 1903."

I remember something about running, like a dream. To this day I cannot remember getting out of that hole or telling Tom Porter, the town's Mountie about our discovery, or anything that happened between. That we did tell Tom I do know, because he got Doc Fletcher, who doubled as the town's coroner, and they went out there and looked for themselves.

The skeleton was there, sure enough, surrounded by all his personal effects, just as I had left him. The back of his head was smashed not by a blow, as I had thought, but by the exit of a large calibre bullet, possibly a forty five. Doc said so, and he found the entry hole near the left temple to prove it.

It was a clear case of murder. And everything Tom Potter could find in that dugout said that this was all that remained of Galen Hawkins, farmer, formerly a constable in the Alberta Provincial Police.

They never did discover who was the Galen Hawkins who had lived on that land near town for almost exactly fifty years. As for me, I have always kept to myself that photo I removed so many years ago from that big white house; only once in a while do I take it out and read the inscription, "To Luke, with love Isobel."